Prepared for Publication
By
HISTORIC PULISHING
San Antonio, Texas
©2017

Autobiography and Reminiscences of John W. Carroll

By

John W. Carroll

LARGE PRINT EDITION

JOHN W. CARROLL.

AUTOBIOGRAPHY AND REMINISCENCES OF JOHN W. CARROLL

LARGE PRINT EDITION

HENDERSON, TENN.
©1898

DEDICATORY.

My only apology for writing whatever may appear on the following pages is that I may leave on record a brief synopsis of my very tame and uneventful life; that my four little grandsons of whom I am very proud, may have an opportunity in after life to take a slight glance at some of the events transpiring in the short life of their paternal grandfather, in the hope that they may improve on my successes (if it can be said that I have had such) and profit by my mistakes which have been many. To them - Raymond Trice Carroll, John Murchison Carroll, Thomas Burns Carroll, and Kirk McKenzie Carroll - the following lines are affectionately dedicated by their grandfather,

JOHN WILLIAM CARROLL.
Henderson, Tenn. August, 1898.

Autobiography and Reminiscences of John W. Carroll

RECOLLECTIONS OF AN UNEVENTFUL LIFE.

CHAPTER I.

My Ancestors.

My great grandfather Carroll immigrated to this country from Ireland many years before the Revolutionary War. Landing in Maryland, the family drifted into North and South Carolina and finally some of them to Tennessee. He and several brothers were in the American army during the entire war, as were also some of his oldest sons. Grandfather Joseph Carroll was about eighty years of age at the close of the Revolutionary War, as he has related to me many times by way of entertainment with many other stirring scenes calculated to live in the tablets of the mind of a small but intensely interested boy. He emigrated to Middle Tennessee in his young manhood, bringing with him five thousand dollars, quite a little fortune for that day and time, where he engaged in farming. Let me say in regard to his character that he was one of those big-hearted, open-handed Irishmen, who loved a dram and occasionally took too much, and when in those happy moods became endorser for other men, which finally nearly exhausted all his means, leaving himself and family in straitened circumstances. (Boys, become surety for no man.)

He soon after emigrated to West Tennessee, settling in Henderson County, then sparsely settled. Here he recuperated somewhat, his lost fortune, but never fully. About this time war was declared by the United States against Great Britain. He immediately volunteered and took part in the battle of New Orleans, Jan. 8th, 1815. It was of great interest to me when a lad to have him relate to me some of the many incidents of camp life and of how he and some comrades on the evening before the battle walked down the line of battle and found one poor fellow down praying and crying, scared almost to death, before there had been a shot fired, and of how they upbraided him for his cowardice; about the death of Gen. Pakenham, the British general, etc. These recitals fired my youthful heart with a burning patriotism and how I wished to wear a uniform; to hear strains of martial music and the roar of cannon; and see glorious war. I thought such things would never come in my day, but alas! they did. Let the sequel tell.

Of my mother's people I knew but little, save that they immigrated to this country shortly after the Revolutionary War from Scotland. My mother's maiden name was Susan Ann Burns, a

Christian woman in deed and in truth, small in stature never weighing as much as one hundred pounds in her life; afflicted always after I knew her, but ever cheerful, always looking well to the wars of her household. She ate not the bread of idleness.

My mother's eldest brother, Samuel Burns, was elected Major of a volunteer battalion to go to New Orleans with Gen. Jackson, but, arriving at the place of rendezvous too late, he with his command, was among the number that were refused, owing to the great number of men offering their service. Many were turned away sadly disappointed.

My father, William Carroll, was born in Lincoln County, Tennessee, and came to Henderson County, Tennessee, where he lived and died. He was a farmer all his life, never held an office but twice, once Justice of the

Peace and for two years Tax Collector of his county, being elected to these positions by votes of his fellow citizens. In politics, always a Democrat. What might be called a rugged man, to principle he adhered with all the tenacity of his nature. Of a mean, low trick he was never guilty; principle was all with him. To the appeals for help from the widow and orphan, his hand was ever open; of his small means he contributed freely to those in distress.

CHAPTER II.

My Immediate Family.

The writer of these pages was born in Henderson County, Tennessee, Nov. 28th, 1841, near 57 years ago. My earliest recollections of life are those of absolute pleasure, associated as they are with the remembrance of one of the kindest of mothers, a father who looked after my interest, a doting grandfather, who lived just across the farm half a mile from our house, who had me believe I was one of the grandest of boys, two grandmothers who thought I was quite a hero generally, one of whom, Grandmother Burns, made her home part of the time at my father's house. Here I was not scolded or petted but dealt with as though I were a real gentleman, which I appreciated very much. When I did wrong, which I frequently did, the matter was discussed with me as one of the auditors and frequently I thought before the conversation ended that, should I be naughty again, grandpapa, whom I dearly loved, would hardly ever speak to me again. Thus I was deterred from a repetition, but perhaps did other mischief equally wrong.

Of our immediate family there were seven children - three boys and four girls - I, being the eldest; J. C. Carroll of this county, next; Dr. J. R. Carroll, now of this town, youngest. Of my sisters, Martha the eldest, many years since dead; Emily next, now living; Cynthia Ann died five years ago; Virginia, the youngest, died in infancy.

My earliest friendship, outside of our own little family, was for a little black-haired, black-eyed girl of about my age - five summers. She came with her mother frequently to visit at my father's house; welcome guests indeed were they, especially to me. Puss Grissom was her name and a dear little child of sweet disposition and gentle manners. Such delightful romps and such happy hours I have seldom, if ever, experienced since. My mind runs back to those happy hours when the watchful care of our mothers was upon us, when the sins and sophistries of the world were unknown to us. And to them I hope troubles are still unknown. When I think of these things, I am reminded of a saying of the Master: "Suffer little children to come unto me, and forbid them not: for of such is the kingdom of Heaven. " Well do I remember on one occasion that this friend and I wandered along down the spring branch that ran from my grandfather's spring, gathering wild flowers as we went, which grew luxuriantly and of rare fragrance all along the banks of the tiny rill. We traveled on gathering flowers until we were lost, but fortunately for us we did not know it; for we did not remember how we had come. Our barefooted tracks in the sand told of our ramble and led to our safe return. Soon after this her father moved away to some other country, which gave us sadness, but happily for us only such as passed quickly away. We have never met since, probably never will, but, wherever she is, in whatsoever clime, I hope she is happy. I remember vividly her merry laughter, her gentle voice; yet, it has been more than fifty years since we parted.

My next very dear friendship was formed in this way: A little boy, a little older than I, visiting my father's house one day, brought with him as a present for me a square-plait whip - the first thing of the sort I had ever seen and of which I was very proud. Such a present and such a friend! He was a noble, brave, generous, manly boy and thank God he is living today - August, 1898. Having known him all these years, I can truthfully testify that he has borne out in manhood those noble traits of character exhibited in his youth and occupies now, as then, a place second to no one in my esteem. On my first visit to his home he treated me most royally; he led me into the mysteries of crawling through the fence cracks and how to turn my head to one side so as not to hurt my nose and how to catch and ride wild cattle - that is - as far as we were able to sit on them, which was but a short distance at a time, being thrown almost as often as we mounted. As we grew up, our friendship was never cooled but rather intensified - my father having moved nearer to where his father lived. We were ever afterwards friends. We helped roll logs together, husk the corn, etc. We both entered the Confederate army in 1861 -

he, in one regiment and I, in another. After the war we played on the violin together, worked in the fields during the days we could, lay in the woods and guarded our horses at night to protect them from the tories who nightly prowled around the premises of Southern men to see if there was any chance to steal. Later we were partners in business; always Democrats; always friends. Such friendships as these, being mutual, are beneficial and always worth cultivation. Never to betray a trust reposed in either nor to go back on a friend has been a part of our motto, and has been religiously and sacredly lived up to by both of us. This good friend was J.N. Galbraith now of Center Point, Tennessee.

CHAPTER III.

My First Home.

During the sixth year of my age my father, owning no land where he lived, purchased a small tract about four miles away, which was a primeval forest, near which place lived Esq. Jno. H. Galbraith. Preparations for a move began right away and consisted in my father going on the place, axe in hand, cutting away the timber and making sufficient opening to set a house. This done, he began felling small trees, eight to ten inches in diameter, cutting them off at required length, hauling them to the selected spot, inviting the neighboring citizens to help to raise the house; a dinner was prepared and sent to the place, and a gallon of whiskey completed the arrangements. On each of the four corners of the house was a man whose duty it was to notch the logs down, one upon another, being handed to them by other men who were on the ground; thus the work proceeded, interspersed with much good feeling, and friendly jests until the last log was put up. Then one piece was put upon either end of the house extending about 24 inches out from either side; on the outer end of this, on either side, was placed a long pole called an abutment, against which the ends of the boards were to rest. Then the pieces on the ends were shorter and shorter to the top. Now we were ready for the boards which were laid on, and a pole of sufficient weight put on them to hold them down and so on to the top; then we began and chopped into the logs of the house on each side and hewed them down thus taking off the rough bark; this done, we proceeded to nail boards on the inside of the cracks between the logs and to fill up the outside of the openings with mud; this done, we had a warm cabin; we then began laying the floor which was made usually of puncheons hewn out and put down as closely as could be done with a hand axe; next, long riven boards were gotten out and shaved as smoothly as possible and a door shutter made of them hung on wooden hinges, which usually made a loud creaking noise on being opened or closed. The place for a fire was usually four to six feet wide, built upon the outside with logs and laid on the inside with mortar and rocks, the hearth back and all up to where the chimney proper started, which was built of sticks and mud. This completed, our humble mansion was ready for occupancy. We had no saw mills then as now, driven by steam, nor nails with which to fasten down boards or plank. Such things of course were in use, I suppose, in some places, but for lack of money on our part did not extend to us. We moved in and began making rails and building a rail fence around the house. We built a log stable for a horse a smoke-house for our meat and a log house for a corn crib, and dug a well. By the time this was all done, it was springtime - March. Father went to clearing a piece of land and I, to piling brush, being the eldest and only help at this time. Late in the season we succeeded in getting six acres of land cleared and planted in corn which of course made only a poor crop on account of the shade being too dense to admit the growth of corn hence the yield was small. However we continued to clear land and build till father had a good small farm of rich land for that section. Thus in course of time better buildings took the place of our primitive log cabin. We were possibly as happy as if our surroundings had been better, that is, we children; for this was all we knew. The labor which we did, though hard, was no particular hardship to us, as we knew nor thought of anything else.

CHAPTER IV.

My First School.

About my eighth year I started for school, father leading the way, axe in hand, cutting off a limb here and a brush there. I blazed a tree first on one side and then on the other, of the newly made path, that brother and I might have a guide to and from the school. (This school generally lasted from ten to twelve weeks. At least from the time we got through our crops until time to take the fodder, we were continuously in school.) On arriving at the Seminary we found quite a pleasant-looking gentleman in charge - Mr. R. G. Hughes, who proved to be what his appearance indicated, a real good fellow. Those who wished to, studied; those who did not relish studying, were not compelled.

Our school building was as primitive as our residence. Round logs composed the body of the house; it had a dirt floor or rather no floor at all; a large fire-place occupied almost one entire end of the building. Round logs had been split open in the middle, the splinters hewn off on the split side, holes bored in from the bark side, and long pins, put in them from that side as supports, furnished the seats for the pupils. These seats were from some cause always made high so that many of the small children's feet reached no nearer the floor, than from six to eighteen inches. There we sat and swung our feet from morning until noon and from noon until dismissal. Our writing desk consisted of one long plank put up on pins along one side of the house; one of the long benches being used for a seat, and of extra height; a log was cut out of the house just over the writing bench to admit the light. Many were the little notes we passed and slipped into each other's copy books while learning to write. At school, we all spelt aloud and read aloud; sometimes we could have been heard two hundred yards away, especially on Friday evenings when we had a spelling match, which was an evening of great excitement and looked to with much interest. Not much school, you think, which is true, as compared with the older communities, or with our modern colleges, built of brick, warmed by hot air and lighted by electricity but then it was a school, the best we had, and did much good. I attended this school three sessions from eight to twelve weeks at a time in so many years. During this time I learned to spell and read fairly well and to write a fairly legible hand. I also learned the multiplication table, possibly to add simple numbers, but there was no such thing in our school as a history, geography or English grammar in fact I never saw an English grammar until I was almost grown, hence pass over grammatical mistakes as lightly as possible.

It was the custom of our professor to allow the first who arrived in the morning to recite first that day and many were the mornings that we almost flew in our efforts to be first. Of the girls and boys who attended this school many remained in the country and grew to be stalwart men and women and helped to make the country what it now is.

CHAPTER V.

My First Visit to a Store.

Grandfather came by our house on his way to the store, riding horseback. I mounted on the same horse behind him. On our arrival at the store, I thought I had almost entered a new world and to me it was: such fancy goods, such nice pictures, such nice glassware, etc., and above all such shining tin ware. I had never dreamed of such a beautiful place as this being on earth. I feasted my eyes on the new things while grand- father chatted away with the storekeeper. When ready to leave for home he asked me what I wanted and gave me what I called for - a new tin bucket of which I was very proud and thankful. Encouraged by this adventure, I some time later made another trip to another store with some company and some mode of transportation; this time there was a gentleman playing on a violin, the sound of which was extremely pleasing to me and it looked so easy for the man to play; it just seemed that anyone could do that; so grandfather when he was ready to leave for home asked me in his good-natured broad Irish accent: "Me lad, what do ye want?" I said: "That fiddle, Grandpa." He told the gentleman to hand it to me which he did. Of course I felt supremely happy, but found it would not play for me as it would for the owner; so I did not succeed in making a musician, for which I have no special regrets.

CHAPTER VI.

My School Days, Etc.

During these years of attending Hughes academy, clearing and fencing land, it was necessary for me to take part in all the duties of the household, my mother being always a delicate woman in feeble health a great part of the time confined to the bed, unable to do her work, and father too poor to hire it done. The younger children and I learned early to do all kinds of work - milk the cows, churn the milk, cook a meal of victuals, etc. It was sometimes the case that brother and I would take the clothing of the family to the well and wash them, which we cheerfully did. We sometimes felt a little mortified at seeing other young people of our age pass by in good clothes and happy, while we were bent over the washtub. All this feeling was wrong in us; all labor is honorable, it matters not what it is, and washing being hard work I think boys should assist in doing the work where the family has it to do. Boys are much stronger than girls, as a rule and should always assist their mother and sisters in doing the hard work about the place.

During these years we had another professor at the Hughes academy, Mr. Smith, a good man; and one other, Mr. T. J. Bailey, also a fine man and who prided himself very much upon the correct understanding of Webster's Blue Back Spelling Book. So we were put through again and again and inaccuracies of other teachers printed out. We now entered upon the study of arithmetic, Pike's old work being the standard at that time; it treated mostly of shillings and pence - old English money - a thing obsolete as far as our currency is concerned. So under this professor, studying eight weeks in a year during the summer solstice, in two years I actually got as far as the rule of three, as well as I remember, about the thirtieth page of the book; and here my educational labors ceased. I am just a little sorry that I can not have a photo of this professor. Unfortunately he was very lame, one leg being much shorter than the other; and one eye seemed smaller than the other. Seated upon a high chair, a long black hickory being conveniently near, woe to the child whom the professor caught not spelling or reading aloud, or smiling at the rosy-cheeked girls, or fixing a pin in the seat so that the nest boy might sit upon it. Engaging in any of these to us seemed little harmless pastimes. On such occasions the professor would rise in his chair and pitch that long black hickory at the violater who must pick it up and carry it to the professor and after a few preliminaries square himself and take a whipping, very much to the edification of the school and to the advancement of education in those parts.

Sometime during these years I saw my first book-agent who called at my father's house to spend the night. After supper he exhibited his books. Among the number was Bunyan's Pilgrim's Progress; after looking through it, I was very anxious to own it; but in this case, as in many others, I did not have the money and father never thought it right to charge a man for lodging and horse feed. So after breakfast next morning the agent left and with him my hopes of obtaining a new book. Though after the lapse of several months I found the much coveted volume in the library of a Baptist minister who kindly loaned it to me. I sped home light of heart and footstep too, and gathered in my brush for a light that night; for remember this was before the time of Lucifer matches, sperm candles, or coal oil, at least in our part of the country. For light we made tallow candles, when we had the beef tallow which we could afford to use only on special occasions. For all ordinary occasions we used a lamp made in the potter's shop, having a bowl that held about a pint into which we put hog's lard or any kind of grease. Into this we put a strip of cotton cloth called a wick and lighted this wick at one end; thus we had a dim light, but this we could not always afford as was the case in this instance; hence the gathering of the sticks and limbs. And now for the reading of the much prized book which began immediately, and let me say, right here and now, that never before nor since, neither do I ever expect to read anything with half the interest as I did this one volume; it held me spellbound until late hours at night. Its stirring scenes passed through my dreams; it riveted my susceptible mind to its passing scenes as with rivets of steel from which I could not and did not want to free my mind, until I had read the last word. Someone who may read this scrawl, will want to know why of such deep interest in such a work. Reader, let me tell you - I had never been fifteen miles from home in my life; I had never read fiction; I had never seen a geography; I knew nothing of fiction and every word my father and mother said to me I believed with all my heart; they never deceived me about anything, hence I accepted as a literal fact everything heard or read; I verily believed that there were somewhere in the world just such roads, such country, as therein described, just such personages as Christian, Patience, Charity and others; such mountains with great gulches through which they had to pass; great lions lying beside the wayside looking for prey; and lo, when

they approached nearer they found
them with chains around their mouths.
Of course I learned later the true intent
of the story, but the reader can see the
cause of my intense interest in the
book.

Along about this time some parties
put up a store about three miles from
our home and advertised that they
would exchange goods for "sang," a
medicinal herb that grew spontaneously
in our neighborhood. I concluded at
odd times to dig some of the roots, this
being the part of the plant used. So in a
little while I had quite a little sack full
of it. In a few days opportunity offered
and I took my "sang" to market and
very readily made a sale. My chief
desire was for store goods enough to
make me a pair of pants and this being
the second store I had ever been in,
everything looked pretty to me, and
noticing a piece of striped goods I

concluded it was the thing I wanted, so
I took the worth of my produce in the
same striped goods, which I learned
later was a very good article - ticking. I
hurried home, elated over my purchase,
and the prospect of a pair of new pants.
Mother, God bless her memory, would
not mortify my feelings by saying it
was not desirable goods for the purpose
for which I wanted it, but cut out the
pants and made them for me. So on
Sunday following I donned my new
pants and a new white shirt, every
thread of which, both warp and woof,
mother had made with her own hands,
even to the buttons which were made of
thread alone by mother's own hands.
Thus attired I went to church. Although
my feet were not incased in patent
leather, or leather of any kind for that
matter, I felt no embarrassment not
knowing at that period of my life, as I
learned later, that the harness made the
horse desirable. Any way those were

happy days; whether modern ways will give to the world a better citizenship remains to be seen.

A few more years of clearing land, rolling logs, etc., brought me to the year 1856. Mother's health, which was always poor, had gone almost completely away; she became almost bedfast for the remainder of her life and to add to our troubles, father, while assisting a neighbor to raise a house, had the misfortune to have his leg broken below the knee. We made a litter and neighbors brought him home, one man at each of the four corners. To further add to our troubles, as though we did not yet have enough, brother, next younger than I and the two oldest sisters were taken sick of typhoid fever. I, being the only one of the family old enough and well enough to do anything, all this was more than I could do, but we secured the aid of a good lady and by the assistance of kind neighbors, which we always had, we did pretty well. Father recovered after a long time as did also brother and sisters, but our poor mother gradually sank. Physicians administered to her the best they could, but she gradually wasted away from the ravages of that awful disease known as consumption of the bowels. She spent her life for the good, upbuilding, consolation, support, and encouragement of her husband and children; many were the times that I heard her encouraging words to my father in the days of our family afflictions, telling him to fear not; the Lord would provide; counseling us children as how we should live and act. She, feeling and knowing that the end was near, gave to her expressions a deep, fervid, intense interest that they would not otherwise have had.

She had always managed, some way, to clothe, mostly with the work of her own hands her family, especially the children; cotton goods for the summer and woolen linseys and jeans for the winter, dying the woolen goods with the bark of the walnut tree which gave a beautiful dark brown color and made it very pretty. The buttons for these goods she made by covering a piece of leather or gourd with some dark material. She lived as the Scriptures describes, a good mother. She looked well to the ways of her husband. I gave to her in her sickness my best attention, while she was sick, and as the other members of the family who were sick grew better I came more and more to the assistance of my mother, but alas! the end came on the evening of March 27th, 1857. She called me to the bedside and told me she was dying: the three next children being unable to go to her, father with difficulty being at the bedside. She uttered a short prayer, pressed us to her dying breast and said to me "John, you have been a dutiful son. Meet me in heaven." Then a few feeble words to father and me to care for her children and all was over. We carried her remains to the family cemetery where they were decently interred: I, being the only member of the family who was able to go to the grave. Returning home, everything was sad and lonely; mother gone, the family sick, but after all our log cabin was **our home.** To care for the sick was my duty which I did as faithfully as I could. The deep interest I felt in them and my knowledge of their gradual and permanent improvement caused a more hopeful spirit to come over me by soon seeing them all able to be stirring a little in the house. Spring being now well advanced, I went about making a small corn crop. So after a few weeks I had it planted; later along father and brother got able to help me some and after all we made a fair crop, a sustenance. Boys, let me say right here, be good to mother; she it is who will go down to the very death for you, she it is who will never forsake you; father, brothers, sisters, aye, even your wife, but mother never: though a felon's chains might bind your hands (which God forbid), the world pass by and scoff, but mother will be there to plead, to comfort, to counsel and to console. Boys, stand by mother, she may become old and fretful and possibly hard to please, but hold up her hands and steady her trembling, tottering steps.

Boys, the prettiest sight that was ever witnessed in the town of Henderson, Tennessee, was that of a young Mr. Savage of that place whose mother was old and tottery; but in that manly son who was then about twenty-two years of age, she had a treasure, a son of whom any mother would be proud. Each Sabbath morning he took mother's arm and supported her feeble steps to the church, sat with her during the service, led her back to her arm chair at her own fireside; thus he preferred mother to all the gayety of society. That young man occupies a lucrative position in one of the learned profession in one of the best cities of the South, and well he should - he deserves it. **Boys, take care of mother.**

During these ten years our wooded country had improved much. Esq. John H. Galbraith was a neighbor, a prominent citizen and afterwards sheriff of our county. D. M. McCollum settled about two miles north of us, a very intelligent and good man and, by the way, the first postmaster we had in our vicinity. Several families moved in from North Carolina and quite a number of families from Middle Tennessee; among whom I remember the families of McCollums, Van Dyke, Bunch, Puryear, Owens, Hardeman, Smith, and others whom I do not now recall settled on the south side of our little neighborhood, bringing with them money with which they purchased lands and paid for them. Also negro slaves which were put immediately to clearing the land which was very rich. The sons of some of these gentlemen worked also in all the labors of the farm. A country store was erected in one mile of my father's house, a postoffice - Center Point - established. School facilities were improved. Sabbath schools were organized; churches, erected; newspapers began to circulate freely among our people. An era of prosperity had come down upon us. Also during these years a Masonic Hall was erected, a two- story frame building; a Masonic lodge organized which occupied the second story of the building, the basement story being used for preaching, open alike to all denominations of Christians and later for school purposes and for all purposes of gathering when the people of the neighborhood thought it necessary to come together. Also during these years the voices of many distinguished statesmen were heard among us; among the number being Hon. J. D. C. Atkins and Emerson Ethridge, who were perhaps the peers of any men in Tennessee upon the political issues of the day; loud and long were the cheers given to each champion as he would score a point against the other, but after the contest was over all returned to their daily avocations with good will for all. Let me say right here that there was not a saloon in our good neighborhood, nor one allowed; neither is there one nor one allowed even to this day, it being more than fifty years since my father, J. H. Galbraith, and other good citizens moved into and began to settle up the country. One fellow, however, had the audacity to attempt to run a saloon over the protest of this good citizenship, which lasted about four days. His goods were not destroyed nor his person injured, but he became aware that it was perhaps safest and best for him to take his whiskey and himself and remove to neighborhoods which were more congenial, which he accordingly did, very much to the satisfaction of all concerned. Just here it is well to remember that whenever a community determines to put an end to a nuisance of that kind, it is best to listen and take heed, for it is going to be done at any cost.

I forgot to say in the proper place, but will now say, that Mr. C. W.

Brooks was one of the first settlers, a good and substantial citizen, always found working for the best interests of the community. Dr. J. F. McKenzie, a man of good mind, great energy, and of much moral worth to the community, also settled in the immediate neighborhood. Three miles west of us lined Mr. John Criner, an old settler and a man of much deep, common sense.

During this period of life I read the newspapers which were full of the happenings in Kansas Territory. The territorial government had applied to Congress for statehood in the Federal union. The abolitionists of the north wanted it admitted only upon the terms of a free state, while the Southern or pro- slavery people wanted it admitted as a slave state; that is, that a citizen of the United States, owning slaves, should have the right to go into Kansas and have his property and slaves protected, as any other property, which had been done under the constitution of the United States from the beginning of the government. The northern Free Soilers, as they called themselves, sent men and arms to Kansas under the name of the Secret Aid Society, for the purpose of driving out the Southern people. The other side being equally determined, it resulted in frequent collisions at arms between the contending factions. My sympathies naturally went out to the Southern people, not that I owned any property in slaves, but I naturally loved the Sunny South together with all her institutions, then as now; whether right or wrong, was no question with me. I am for her and will be, I think, while I have an existence upon the earth. My patriotism began to run pretty high; so I made up my mind that if I had any way of getting over there I would go and help my people. After some reflection I frankly laid the matter before my father, telling him of my intentions. He heard me kindly through my story. When I had finished, he told me that I knew nothing of life in an army; that I had best wait, for he believed that inside of two years a fearful war would be forced upon the people of the Southland; that, when the time came, it would be our duty to aid our people to the best of our ability. After this conversation I abandoned the idea of a trip to Kansas.

CHAPTER VII.

My Civil War Experience.

About this time came John Brown's raid into Virginia. Thus every move on the political chessboard was a move in the direction of war the most fearful in the annals of history. Thus John Brown's raid was the first shot fired and the first onslaught made upon the institutions of our country, which burst upon us in all its fury in the year 1861. I was then in my nineteenth year; full of patriotism and hope of success; anxious to take part in the struggle, I enlisted in a company being raised by Richard Barham May, 1861. The company was soon recruited to about one hundred men. Barham was elected Captain and a full quota of officers were selected. We went into camp at Trenton, Tenn. I was elected fourth corporal, the lowest office in the army, if it could be called an office at all. But what of that; any and all were willing to serve anywhere! To wear a Confederate uniform and fight for one's country was glory enough, we thought. If positions were offered, they were accepted patriotically and the muskets were carried with the same pride and patriotism that actuated a Major General.

We drilled every day - morning and evening, attended roll call, did camp duty, cooked our own rations, washed our own clothes, etc.

Our first lieutenant being a man who had some military training, we were soon a fairly well drilled company of volunteers.

I bought a copy of Hardee's Tactics, also a copy of military law and by adding study to practice, pretty soon became a fair drill-master. In the volume in military law I learned that the rules and discipline of an army was no Sunday school affair. Soon we had companies enough in camp to organize a regiment - 27th Tenn. Infantry. C. H. Williams was elected Colonel. Then began company, batallion and regiment drills, in earnest; officers drills also. These drills with other duties occupied all our time. About this time it occurred to the powers that were, that we had neglected to elect a chaplain, which had to be done, as everything else in that patriotic regiment, by the votes of the soldiers. So a young man applied for the position and went among the different companies soliciting votes and I for very mischief went out among the companies not knowing them nor they me, but few outside our own company. Other mischievous comrades caught on and went out electioneering for me; the election came off and I was actually elected chaplain of one of the finest regiments in the Confederate service. When the result was announced I was actually dumbfounded. The colonel ordered the new chaplain to appear at headquarters. I positively refused to go and after an explanation by some friends that the whole thing was a huge joke on my part and never intended to go outside of my own company, the matter was dropped. I never afterward attempted to play the role of preacher.

Soon after this I was elected orderly sergeant of our company. We then went to Columbus, Ky.; thence to Felicanna, Ky.; then to Bowling Green. Ky.: then to Nashville, Tenn.; thence to Corinth, Miss.

At this place, our first lieutenant, John Skiffington, concluded that a position in the quartermaster's department would be more in keeping with his ideas of war. He resigned his commission as Lieutenant and I was elected to fill his place.

At this time General Albert Sidney Johnston who was in command of the Confederate army, ordered a move upon the Federal army, under the command of Gen. U. S. Grant, which was encamped on the west side of the Tennessee river at Pittsburg Landing and around Shiloh church from which the battle took its name. We moved out on Thursday evening and on Friday evening encountered the federal outpost. After a light skirmish we drove them in. On Saturday we lay in line of battle all day long and Saturday night also. This delay was caused by the tardiness of one division of the army not getting in position, as it should have done, until late Saturday evening.

So on Sunday morning, April 6th, 1862, the sun rose brightly; everything was full of animation, life, and hope.

We moved to the attack driving everything before us; cheer after cheer went up as we drove them from one position to another. So by five o'clock p.m., having fought all day, we had the federal army in our clutches; but just at this juncture, Gen. Buell of the federal army began to land his army of reinforcement on the west bank of the river, consisting of forty thousand men. There was also a powerful federal fleet in the river that bombarded us all night long on Sunday night. With this reinforcement they succeeded in driving us off the field by three o'clock on Monday evening. The combined loss of both - armies is placed at forty thousand men - a fearful slaughter. Of the many little incidents that happened during the two days battle I will only relate one or two. Captain Barham being slightly wounded early in the engagement, retired from the field. The command of the company then devolved upon me, as first lieutenant. A member of the company came to me after the battle had been raging for some hours on Sunday morning and told me he was going to be killed. He looked pale, though fearless. I tried to dissuade him but, nay; he said it would be so. I asked him to take some tobacco with me, which he did, saying it would be his last, which it was; the poor fellow was killed a few minutes afterwards.

On the battlefield there was a pretty large highland pond and is today denominated by the federals as the "Bloody Pond," and is so marked. Well do I remember wading through it on Sunday evening about four o'clock, the water coming to my waist. The federals were making a strong fight here; knowing that if I were wounded and should fall in this water I would drown, I rushed through and waited until the company came up. We passed on beyond this place to near the bank of the river, and at dusk a cannonball from a federal gunboat cut off the whole top of a tree which fell lengthwise on our regiment and killed eleven men of one company. Darkness now closed the scene and on Monday evening, after fighting all day to 3 p.m., we returned to Corinth, Miss. We were worn out and disconsolate; so many comrades, who had gone out with us, were not there to answer roll-call as they had been left wounded or dead on the battlefield. Our ranks were so depleted that a reorganization of the whole army was necessary. I was chosen Captain of our company. Of such distinction I was much pleased and very thankful as I regarded this as an endorsement of my conduct in my past life (with the company as well as my patriotism).

The ordeal of battle and reorganization having been gone through with, we began drilling daily. More regard was paid to discipline. In a short time however the federal army began to move against us. Sharp, close, hard-picked fighting continued night and day with occasional fighting with considerable bodies of both armies; notably at Farmington, a village town between Corinth and Pittsburgh Landing. In May, however, the army evacuated Corinth and moved round to Chattanooga, Tenn., from there to Mumfordsville, Ky., where a portion of the army captured the federal garrison; then to Richmond, Ky., where the federal army was defeated, and to Perryville where was fought one of the hardest battles of the war, in which I was wounded. A ball passing across and cutting out a piece of the right knee cap, from which I did not recover rapidly. From there I was taken to

Knoxville, Tenn., over a rough road in a wagon. On the way out some one stole my hat and coat also my haversack containing my provisions. Arriving at Knoxville, Oct. 17, we were surprised to find ourselves and the whole earth covered with a four inch snow. At this place General Manney visited me. On the next night we were loaded on a freight train and started to Chattanooga.

Here I want to turn aside to relate an incident of two members of my company: William Rhodes of Lexington, Tenn., one of the nicest young men in the regiment and as brave as he was young and fair; and Frank Buck, a mere boy, both of whom came to me when we were in line of battle and told me they were going to be killed that day. Their pale features, their calm demeanor, their determined looks impressed me much. While I had no authority to offer such thing, yet, I did offer that they take pass and drop out, which they refused to do and were both killed in less than two hours; I wish to relate here the conduct of Joe Wheeler, of Henderson county, the color-bearer of the regiment and a member of my company, who, while holding the colors aloft during the hottest of the fight, had his right arm shattered, let the colors fall, but, seizing them with the other hand, held them up until a bullet through his brain put an end to his existence.

Arriving at Chattanooga about midnight, the weather at this time being very cold, we were unloaded and carried to a frame church on the outskirts of the city and laid on the floor as we arrived, until the floor was literally covered with wounded men, few of whom had blankets to cover with and no chance for a fire to warm.

We were in anything but a comfortable condition. This was the best, I suppose, that could be done for us; any way it was hard luck. During the night owing to poor health I found it necessary to dispense with what clothing I had left, except one shirt which I had on. Morning soon dawned and some friends of mine found me in a nude condition and ministered unto my necessities. A brother whom I had not seen for months came walking up, having heard of the battle, and wanted to see me. Soon I had comfortable clothes. A good room in the hotel and a bed to lie on; what a great thing to have a friend! Boys, never betray a confidence reposed in you nor go back on a friend.

Bragg's army moved to Shelbyville, Tenn., where another reorganization of the army was necessary and our ranks were by this time very much depleted. I of course was absent on wounded furlough and it was not expected that I would again be able for military duty. I was left out of the organization, but after months I became able for duty again as a cavalryman. I reported for duty, was transferred to the cavalry department and ordered to West Tennessee, then overrun with the federals, there to raise a company of cavalry which I did after several weeks and many narrow escapes.

While in Middle Tennessee I met with my old time friend and neighbor, J. N. Galbraith, who had been released from a northern prison, having suffered much and lost the use of one eye. I had sufficiently recovered from the wound to travel with the aid of a stick. We decided to try our luck in crossing the Tennessee river and trying to see home-folks again. We succeeded in evading the federals, arriving at home and spent a brief time very happily. In a couple of days it was discovered that we were at home and reported to the authorities who gave us a hot chase and came near capturing both of us. On arriving at the Tennessee river on our return to protection, we found no means of crossing, but we turned into a deep gulch covered with a thick underbrush and tied our horses, disrobing ourselves of clothing except a couple of undergarments, and procuring a couple of logs, making them fast together with grape vines, we pushed into the river and used our best exertions to make the opposite shore before some federal gunboat should overhaul our frail craft and take us to prison. 'All went well until we came half across the river; the grape vines came untied; the logs rolled apart and we were into the river. Both of us being good swimmers we went on pretty well. On nearing the bank I asked my friend how he was doing; he answered pretty well, only one leg was cramped and sticking straight down. However, we went ashore, rested a little, held a council of war and decided to move on to a farm house which we did. Placing ourselves behind a fence with our heads just over the top rail, we called. A lady came to the call. Making known to her our situation she soon found us friends. With a skiff we soon succeeded in crossing our horses and getting on the remainder of our clothing which we very much needed. That night we spent under the friendly boughs of a spreading oak.

On my return to West Tennessee for the purpose of raising a company of volunteers, we had many difficulties. We had no arms except occasionally a flint-lock shotgun that we could pick up. We went along, enrolled whom we could and let them remain at home.

This enrollment was secretly carried on until such a time as we could get men enough to organize a company, which we finally succeeded in doing. Our company when organized consisted of about sixty men. So on a summer day of 1863, at a good spring in a deep hollow, on the farm of J. T. Maness, the organization was perfected. I was elected Captain of this company also, M.L. Cherry, first lieutenant, William Record and Robert Long, second lieutenants. We had now men enough to start South but no arms or ammunition. We however concluded to try a raid down towards Adamsville, where we were sure there were federal soldiers of the "home- made sort," as we termed them. (That is persons who, living in this country, had joined the federal army.) Capt. James Stinnett, who had a small company, and I, with what armed men I had, went down and sure enough we came on a good sized company of them. A fight immediately occurred in which we were successful by putting them to flight, capturing a few of them and getting one of our men wounded. Getting a few guns we returned somewhat encouraged, bivouaced in the woods a few days and concluded to raid a portion of the country known as Hooker's Bend, where was congregated a lot of thieves claiming to be, and were, federal soldiers, who would make frequent incursions into our part of the country and carry off whatever they could get their hands on. Here we found a formidable company, but who seemed not disposed to fight much. So after maneuvering most all day, three of our boys being hungry rode up to a house, asked to get some bread and were closed in upon and captured by the federals and carried to their camps for the night. Following closely after them we remained until daylight and made a rush for them. One of the prisoners, a Mr. Benson, just as day began to break seeing the guard turn his head away, gave him a blow with his fist, that sent the fellow whirling to the ground and made his escape. Meeting him he told us where they had camped; so we charged upon them and as usual they fled. We recaptured our soldiers, picked up several horses and a few guns, captured a few prisoners and ran the crowd into the bottom, returning again to our places of hiding, not knowing what hour a heavy column of federals might come upon us.

During these days, Col. Faulkner of a Kentucky batallion of Confederates passed through the country whose advance guard were dressed in federal uniform in order to protect themselves and evade the federal columns, should they meet them. Calling at the house of a unionist they inquired of him if there were any rebels in the country; he said there were and proceeded to give names, writing them down for the officers, noting as he wrote what should be done to this one and to that one. When he came to the name of my father, he said burn him out, that he had a son in there who was a bad guerrilla, referring to me. When he had finished his memorandum, the officer told him to get over the fence and move along that these were Confederates he was talking to. The mortification and downright fear depicted in his face was awful to behold. They put him under guard, foraged on him taking bacon, hams, chickens, etc., and he furnished a bountiful supply. During the night the officer sent for me and, when I arrived, had the man brought into my presence and rehearsed in my presence what the old sinner desired done with his southern neighbors. I saw that those men intended to kill him; they told him they would. Having known the old rascal for years, I begged for his life and offered to go security for his good behavior during the war. He promised to leave the country and not to meddle again in such manner, which he did and kept his word faithfully with me. And after peace was made he made a warm personal friend of mine. At his death I was one of the pall- bearers and helped to place his remains in their last resting place. Peace to his ashes!

Our desire now was to get out through the federal lines to Mississippi, where we could get arms. There being six other pieces of companies in the country, we got together and organized by electing D. T. Spain, Colonel; James Franklin, Major, and had altogether, perhaps, three hundred men, mostly unarmed and in constant danger of being captured, frequently having to disband and seek safest in the woods. At this time General N. B. Forrest forced his way through the federal lines and came to Jackson, Tenn. We immediately reported for duty to General Forrest and went South into Northern Mississippi. A great many men of our number had once belonged to the Southern army who, at the time of the evacuation of Corinth, Miss., after the battle of Shiloh, were at home and who remained there until this time. Here a new trouble arose; a report was circulated to the effect that these men would be returned to their old commands in infantry service and their horses used to mount new men. This caused a regular stampede; men left in dozens until within a short time there were only 150 men present out of the 300 taken out; this necessitated a reorganization. I was absent at the time, but the whole batallion was thrown into one company and I retained as captain of it. I was surprised on my return and of course felt grateful for the honor. We were then attached to a regiment, 21st Tenn. Cavalry, under Col. A. ST. Wilson who by the way was a brave and chivalrous man. Our first introduction to the federals now was a skirmish in the night-time which was pretty exciting, but no damage either way. A couple of days later we met a federal force at Okolona, Miss., who fought us hard but we whipped them and drove them into Memphis, capturing and killing many of them and getting arms and ammunition of war enough to arm our command; also a lot of blankets which we very much needed; many of us not having even one blanket nor an overcoat. Returning to Okolona we rested a few days. The winter being very severe it was with difficulty that we kept from frost-bites which some did not. Getting the command in as good shape as possible, we moved to Jackson, Tenn., capturing Trenton, Tenn., and other places, fighting at Johnsonville on the Tennessee river, Paducah and Fort Pillow on the Mississippi river, which was a garrison of negro troops commanded by white men. After much parleying and urging a surrender to us they refused; we stormed the works and when the fight was over and the smoke cleared, there was not many of them left. We carried off the artillery and what prisoners we had taken. Just here I will state that, while the flag of truce was up, Captain James Stinnett and I with some picked men crawled up close under the guns to be ready in case they refused to surrender, to prevent them from discharging their cannon into our ranks which we successfully did. The little town was then by some mishap or other burned. This being in April, 1864, we had not tents or other shelter. During all these winters when it rained we protected ourselves as best we could with oilcloths captured from the federals; our head we pillowed on our saddles when we had time for a nap; our rations were poor; musty corn meal, and bacon and beef when we could get it. Of this we did not complain. It was the best the Confederacy could do for us. Our currency was so much depreciated as to be almost worthless. To give an idea of its purchasing power, I owned a good horse which would, in ordinary times, be worth a hundred dollars, which horse was valued into the service at eighteen hundred dollars. Tobacco was worth five dollars for a single plug and, if fine, about twenty dollars; a large watermelon would bring from five to ten dollars. I saw sixty dollars paid for one quart of whiskey. Of this currency we did not have very much; we were not paid regularly. I remember that at the time of the surrender the government owed me about twenty-seven hundred dollars. The wages paid an officer of my rank was one hundred and thirty dollars per month; hence you will observe that I had not been paid in quite a while. Of this we made no complaint, as one was about as well off without it as with it. The success of the cause was our leading thought and, for the accomplishment of this end, we were willing to undergo anything that might befall us.

Returning from this digression to the thread of my theme, we left Fort Pillow, denuded of me and guns, and West Tennessee with not a federal command in it outside of the city of Memphis. Turning again Southward we crossed the Tennessee river at Florence, Ala., crossing the men in skiffs and on flat boats, and swimming the horses; no wagons except those for carrying ammunition and a few ambulances were allowed. Encountering the federals on the east bank of the river, driving on toward Nashville, we hurried them along, stopping at Pulaski, Tenn., taking a few block-houses. This being now well up into the month of May. We passed on to Athens, Tenn., where we forced a surrender of about 2,500 men who were well fortified. General Forrest did this bold strategy very much to our delight; to storm a breastwork across a broad deep ditch and it protected with an abattis made secure with telegraph wire, was no light job. But they knew we had stormed the works at Fort Pillow a few weeks before and had confidence in us to believe that we would do the sanae for them. Passing on we came to a negro corral where were quarters of a large number of negroes and horses belonging to the federal government; all were protected by a block-house and federal garrison. This we captured -

horses, negroes and all, but they were retaken that same evening by the federals, over which we had a skirmish; there being only a few men left as a guard they were not able to cope with the federal forces. Passing on from here we were ordered back west of the Tennessee river to meet a raid of infantry, cavalry, and artillery, commanded by Major-General Sturgess of the federal army. The brigade, Bell's, to which we were attached marched seventy-five miles during the day and night before we encountered them. Striking them at Brice's Cross Roads, Miss., on June 10th, 1861, tired, hungry, and sleepy as we were, we dismounted and made immediate preparations for the assault. Our enemies outnumbering us almost, if not quite, three to one, we knew we had hard work to do. When our brigade arrived, General Forrest met us and had something to say to each man as he passed along the line - some word of encouragement. We could all see with what intense feeling and anxiety he regarded the issue. This made the men more determined. We moved to the assault through a deep underbrush in which the enemy was concealed. The onslaught was terrific and repelled with equal vigor; for hours it seemed as though we were on a scale which rose and fell with about equal regularity as each side charged and countercharged, until finally we broke the center of the federal line and, doubling it back, put them to riot. We followed them until midnight and for nearly two days afterward, killing and wounding many of them, taking many prisoners. In this engagement many of our best men were lost, many killed and many more wounded. After this and our return, we went into camp for a much needed rest for both men and horses, which lasted only about two weeks, until another raid was started out from Memphis under the command of General A. J. Smith of the federal army, a brave and skilful officer, with a more powerful army than that brought out by Gen. Sturgess. About July 10th, 1864, we met at Harrisburg, Miss., and in a charge on the evening before the main battle, our brigade was considerably damaged and forced to retire; many of our men shed tears, this being the first repulse we had met with. During the night the Federals fortified a strong position and on the morning we assaulted them and after two hours were compelled to withdraw from the field and accomplish by strategy what we could not do by main force. Our company on that morning consisted of sixty-two men leaving out the horse holders which were every fourth man. (Remember we fought on foot) and when the fight as over thirty-two were either killed or wounded. A sad day indeed for us, but we had to fight whatever we came to. To drive General Forrest out of Mississippi was, it seemed, the determination of the federal government and not to be driven much we were equally determined. On the next day we, by a flank movement, brought them out of their stronghold and succeeded in driving them from the state after some days of skirmishing. On the third day of this battle the federals, had gotten into a skirt of timber beyond an open field in which were long rows of pens of corn, cotton gins, fencing, etc. All of which they had set on fire. The sun being very hot, the heat and smoke from this burning property was too much for me. I was suddenly overcome by heat and had to be carried from the field. From the effects of which I have never recovered nor never will. On the next day I was able to sit on my horse, but weak and feeble. At this time the

Confederacy was waning fast. Of the six hundred thousand men of all arms, who had enlisted into the service of the Confederacy, at least half; or more than half of them had been killed, wounded, died, or discharged on account of sickness, or deserted. I am sorry to say we had some of this latter class. There could not have been, I do not think, more than 250 to 275 thousand left and they were guarding a line of defense extending from the Atlantic to the Indian Territory on the west. Of the two million eight hundred thousand enlisted in the federal army, we could not have, I think, disposed of more than eight hundred thousand of them; pretty good if we had done this much. Now against the two hundred seventy-five thousand Confederates, there was an army of two million men of the federal army to hurl against that thin line of Confederates. But each day we presented as solid front as possible and fought as gallantly

and as faithfully as in the earlier days
and possibly more so. Another short
rest, shoeing horses and getting ready
for another raid, we were notified of a
force moving out from Memphis again;
this time by the way of Pontotoc, Miss.,
commanded by the same federal, Gen.
A. J. Smith, with a still more
formidable force than before. This was
now August: the weather, distressingly
hot; horses and men jaded, but there
was no chance for a rest. We moved
out in the direction of the invading
force and met them near Pontotoc,
Miss., began skirmishing with them,
prepared for an engagement, but
finding the federal force had infantry
enough to cover our front and us in
single line and as much cavalry as we
had we were utterly unable to force
them back. As we would engage them
in front their cavalry would swing
around to our rear and force us to fall
back. Thus we went for several days

until finally General Forrest resorted to one of his masterly strategic movements. The order was passed through camp for volunteers to go on a heavy detached service and none but good horses allowed to go. So when we were ready, our command was very formidable; neither did we know where we were to go, but the fact was soon developed that we were destined for Memphis. Filing out around the federal army, leaving General Chalmers in command of the forces left in front of the enemy, we went on quietly until we came to Cold Water river, a considerable stream on which we had to lay a pontoon bridge; this we soon did, General Forrest assisting in the work with his own hands. Crossing quietly and night soon coming on, we proceeded on our way and just before day a shot from Captain Bill Forrest's pistol notified us that the federal outpost had been encountered; one guard being killed and the remainder captured. At this signal we made a charge for the city, at the outskirts of which we ran upon a division of federals who had just arrived and gone into camp the previous night. These we run over and through, who in their night-clothes looked like ghosts but to them we paid no attention save to give them a passing shot. each part of our command having been previously assigned to different parts of the city and ordered not to pay any attention to firing either on the right or left. Our part of the command having been ordered to the Gayoso Hotel in which were guarded Gen. Washburn and his staff to effect their capture was our mission. A dense fog overhung the city, making it impossible to distinguish a gray from a blue uniform, which was possibly an advantage to us. On arriving at the hotel we found it strongly guarded and one of the great difficulties now was to find something with which we could batter down the doors. We however succeeded, after some minutes, in getting in but during this time a continual firing was going on upon us from housetops, cellars, etc. Gen. Washburn succeeded in making his way out through some private passage and getting away. However we captured most of his staff officers and also the General's uniform, watch, etc. Not having time for the officers to dress, we had to march them out in their night clothes and barefooted. Of course this was not very elegant, but the weather being warm it did not seem to be injurious to their health. Inside the building there were many hand-to-hand combats, men fighting like demons. This melee lasted, perhaps, an hour and a half. During this time the guards whom we had run over on the outskirts of the town in the early part of the action, had formed in our rear and as they thought effectually closed every avenue of escape for us. This necessitated a charge which we successfully did, fighting pretty hard at times and losing some good men and capturing some prisoners. Darkness still hung over the earth and discerning a line of battle moving into us and being near, Col. Forrest requested me to find out which they were. I rode hastily up to them and asked in a low commanding voice what command. The answer came loudly and distinctly: "Ohio boys." Said I, "All right, " turned and galloped away. This just saved us, as there was a command in front of us then. skirmishing with us; so we turned to the right and galloped out, getting out with the prisoners. General Forrest moved out a couple of miles and formed a line of battle. He sent in a flag of truce and also Gen. Washburn's uniform and asked that the clothing of the captured officers and some provisions be sent them; also proposed an exchange of prisoners. To this Gen. Washburn demurred saving that he would capture Forrest and his whole command before night. General Forrest replied that he would return by way of the Hernando road, the way he had come in, which he did; but Washburn considered this bold assertion a mere ruse, concluding that his enemy had designs on the Memphis and Charleston railroad which was in the hands of the federals from Memphis to near Corinth and accordingly put his forces on that road to protect it from the expected raid. So we proceeded as we came on the same road back to Panola, Miss. This raid into Memphis had the effect of again ridding North Mississippi of a federal army. That which we could not do by fighting, we did by bold strategy.

I will stop to relate that during the war many federal soldiers took wives of the negro women where they were quartered; among our prisoners on this raid was a real fat Dutchman who had a negro wife, whom he carried along with him. The weather being very warm; water, scarce; both captors and captured became very thirsty. On coming to a bold running stream of clear water, our Dutchman rushed in and fell down to drink. A mule (on which some of our soldiers were mounted) standing in the water happened to notice the Dutchman lying behind him, raised one foot and kicked him in the head killing him instantly, at which the negro lamented very much but the procession moved on.

Getting to Mississippi again, we were much worn down - men and horses too. We were compelled to have at least a month's rest after getting in for both man and beast. After getting in as good condition as possible and fully satisfying the federals that we were not going to give up our territory, we moved into Middle Tennessee again and, having a long line to guard, we were continually on the march skirmishing and fighting. Again in Tennessee we encountered federals on every side. Moving on to Pulaski we drove in the pickets and captured the garrison; then to Sulphur Trestle where we had a pretty hard fight, destroying the trestling which was a long one; thence around Columbia, Tenn., burning a bridge and destroying railroad track; at another place we captured a considerable fort and several prisoners; at this point an old Dutchman who was a member of the garrison had dug him quite a hole, reaching in under a steep bluff. After the surrender of the garrison, every effort was made to get this fellow out of his hiding place to no effect; said he had no business out "dare." Being no way to get him except to dig him out, we moved off and had not the time to give to the capture of one man. We next moved in the direction of Lawrenceburg where we had a pretty stiff fight; next in the direction of Franklin, Tenn., where we took part in that memorable battle; after this we were sent to Murfreesboro, Tenn., to assist in the capture of that place. After a hard struggle we failed to capture the works. Here I was severely wounded in the left foot, the ball passing through the instep, from which I have never recovered. I was carried to the field hospital for the purpose of amputating the limb, but after a consultation H was deferred. I was then carried back to Franklin, Tenn., where I remained until Hood's defeat in front of Nashville.

Here I will digress to say that the company was commanded by Lieutenant M.L. Cherry until the army again arrived in Mississippi. Here another reorganization was necessary, made so by the fearful depletion of our ranks. I was again chosen Captain of the company which now took what was left of about three companies to make one. Mr. Frank Bell of Purdy, Tenn., the former adjutant of the regiment, first lieutenant; Mr. W. B. Malone of McNairy county, second lieutenant. I was never with the company again; this being the last of December, 1864, and the surrender occuring in May 1865. I was unable to walk even at the time of the surrender. (Here I want to say that two nobler, braver, officers never lived than Frank Bell and W. B. Malone.)

Leaving Franklin just ahead of the retreating army in a one-horse wagon with one mule to draw it, Mr. James

Record, a member of our company, who had been with me all the while nursing me, drove the mule; I lay on my back with the shoe off the well foot and it placed against the front end of the wagon to hold the wounded foot from jolting against the wagon; the weather being very cold and only one blanket each, we moved out, cold of course; my right foot was soon severely frost-bitten; so much so, that the skin and toe-nails all came off together. In crossing one of those rapid running streams in Lawrence county, Tenn., had to keep a certain track for on either side the water was very deep. Crossing one of these streams the water came up over me. Of course I had my head up above the water; but, on nearing the bank and the current being very strong, our wagon swerved downstream (a few feet perhaps) where the water was very deep. Just before reaching the bank, it seemed that the mule would give way entirely and so stood holding with all his might; with all the encouragement that could be given him, he finally male a supreme effort, got to the bank and out of the water, very much to our delight; for as to me I thought a watery grave was my doom. Continuing our journey my clothes froze on me and I was in quite a bad plight. Calling at a farm house late in the evening we were taken in, warmed and fed. We continued our journey the next day with about the same luck as the previous day, except the wetting. Just here I want to state that lieutenant I. J. Galbraith who had a large mule came to us and put it to the wagon in place of ours, which was about worn out. He rode my horse which was being led behind the wagon; the kindness of this gentleman we much appreciated; it enabled us to go on our journey; he also stayed with us until the end. On the fourth day we arrived at Carrollsville, on the Tennessee river. By this time I was very much worn out but had no chance for a much needed rest and the treatment which I so much needed. Behind us thundered the cannon and shouts of a victorious army; in our front yawned the turbid waters of the Tennessee river upon whose bosom and sometimes, in distinct hearing, floated a portion of the United States navy. To cross we were compelled. Casting about we found a man with a dugout just large enough for me to be laid in and for the oarsman to sit on the other end. The frail craft sinking up to within about four inches of the top. We moved on gently, though the river was level with its banks; the low coarse whistle of a federal gunboat being uncomfortably near; we crossed all right and friends carried me up the bank and to Mr. Frank Hassell's who lived near the river. At this point before crossing, we had to abandon our wagon; the federals having destroyed every kind of craft on the river to prevent people from crossing, there was nothing left but to swim the stock to the west bank. At Mr. Hassell's we were kindly treated that night. Early the nest morning we saw approaching the residence from the direction of the river, a body of men some of whom were wearing blue overcoats. A heavy fog hung over the land as a pall of darkness, making it impossible to distinguish friends from foes. The men who had been with me the evening before and night, feeling themselves unable to cope with the (as we thought) advancing foe, retired. I arose from the bed and holding to a chair managed to get to the gallery in front of the house, and laying my wounded foot on the railing and clasping my left arm around a post, all this time clad in my night-clothes I was watching the approach of the body of men. I thought that death or a prison awaited me and not knowing which, but, if any difference, preferring the former, either of which was most appalling. I had noticed moving about the house, during my stay there over night and that morning, a rather beautiful young lady of medium height, delicate build, dark brown eyes, long flowing tresses of silken black hair, but had not once thought of the real deep, fiery southern blood that coursed her delicate veins until she came suddenly up to where I was holding to the post. She handed me my pistols which had been left in the room and said to me, "Sir, those are federals. Sell your life as dearly as possible. They will burn this house and premises, but that is all right. Kill as many Of them as possible." Saying this she moved inside the door to await results. Being determined never to go to a federal prison and being much encouraged by the words of the young lady, I stood as erect as possible for one in my condition and determined to fire on them with deadly aim. as soon as they came to the fence, which was within about ten feet of where I was standing. When they arrived at the fence to my great surprise and gratification, they were Confederates, many of whom I knew. We had a good handshake all around and were happy. They remarked that from the color of my dress they would have supposed I was for peace.

The name of this young lady I do not now remember, but learned that she is in Paducah, Ky., engaged in the millinery business, doing well and loved and respected. God grant her a long and happy life and an eternity of bliss.

Collecting our little band, taking leave of this kind and hospitable family, Mr. Hassell lending a buggy to assist in getting me home, we started on

our journey again, the distance to
Center Point, the home of my father,
being about thirty miles. Putting my
wounded foot upon the seat of the
buggy by the side of the driver and
laying my head and shoulders in the
foot of the buggy, a peculiar position
for a buggy ride, but it was the best and
only way I could go. This position and
the condition in which my foot had
gotten by this time, made the travel
very painful to me. I surely thought that
I would not survive the day; a rough
and rocky road added to my tortures.
Arriving at my father's house about
dark, I was carried in, given some
nourishment and placed on a feather
bed, a luxury I had not enjoyed for
quite a while. The wound being very
painful, I slept but little, but the fact of
being at home, gave me much cheer.
The wound grew worse all the while, so
much so, that fears were entertained of
lockjaw. I remained at father's one

week only. When it was known among the Unionists that I was at home wounded, that part of the country being largely on the side of the federal authorities, it was dangerous to be seen in many places. I was doomed, so the enemy thought, to capture and possibly death. Suspecting their intentions, a good Southern lady took a piece of cloth, made with her own hands, and went out among the loyal citizens, as they termed themselves; the cloth was suitable for men's wear and offered it for sale; stopping at every house and chatting along with the Union ladies, she soon found the plans they had laid for my capture or death; of course the cloth was not sold nor was it intended to be; it only furnished an excuse for the calls, but I was fully notified of the fact that I was to be dispatched. A brother who was at home had an os wagon backed up to the door of the room and I was duly placed in it and driven, jolting along a distance of four miles, to the home of an aunt of mine who cared for me, giving me all the attention possible. This was Aunt Nancy A. Carroll, whose small baby girl would bring such things to me as she thought I would like to eat and also slip them to me. The physician allowed me only a certain amount which we did not think enough. Here I improved some. In about one week, however, I was again informed that it would be dangerous for me to remain longer. It seemed as if the loyal unionists thirsted for my little remaining blood. So I again sought the ox wagon and this time went to Mr. Jessie Rhodes', a good Southern man and very kind, whose wife was equally kind. Here I was laid behind the door in a room where no one saw me except they came into the room, which they seldom did.

I remained here until the 17th day of the following April. On that day I crawled out into the yard and saw for the first time in four months the beauties of nature. The leaves were green, as were every living thing; wheat, up pretty tall, lambs, frisking about; farmers, at work; all nature wore a smile. I remember that I had only seen through the crack of the door so safely was I hidden. This effort of crawling out, though, damaged me and it was three weeks before I could be out again. But during this last confinement, though I improved rapidly and was able to read, which helped me to while away the time, the wound recuperating all the time. Again getting out I thought by laying my wounded foot on the horse's neck I could ride to father's, a distance of about seven miles, which I did getting along pretty well.

Arriving home, my sisters put my horse away. Stepmother and all the family came out and seated. We were engaged in a good old-fashioned family circle conversation, for neither thay nor I expected, when I was taken away from there the previous winter, that I would ever be home again. In the midst of this pleasant reunion what should I see but a company of bluecoats, about forty in number, near the house and approaching rapidly. Escape was impossible even if I had been well; a bold front was my only chance and that a very poor one. I thought, when I learned that it was a troop of the famous 6th Tenn. Cavalry, U.S.A., Col. Hurst's, noted for their chivalry in killing prisoners, robbing houses, wardrobes, etc., a terror i n fact to old men, helpless women and innocent children who happened to be a Southern turn of mind. I took up my crutches, hopped out to the gate, put my crippled foot on the fence, addressed them as gentlemen, invited them to alight which they declined to do. Just here the strategy on my part began. My belief has ever been that they intended to kill me as their custom usually was on such occasions. Inquiring my name and rank, and being told, they began to question me upon a great many things, my wounds, my horse, and many other things; I answered to the best advantage. Finally of them, a large stout man wearing a pair of green spectacles, rode up near where I was standing with a pistol in hand. I believed my time had come. Just at his moment one of the c rowd spoke up and said: "That man is telling the truth," referring to me. After a consultation with each other they turned to me and said they wanted my horse. To this I replied I had no horse, having lost him when I was wounded; my horse that moment was in the stable. They then proposed to take me to prison. To this I, of course, consented, telling them as I had nothing and could not ride they would have to haul me. They then inquired the way to several different homes of Southern families which I proceeded to give them, though in a very circuitous route, telling them as I could not get away I would be there on their return to which they assented and rode away. One may imagine, but not realize, how supremely happy I was at this. My great fears were that they would look about the barn and see that my statements were false but they did not. I watched the receding column with breathless anxiety, as it slowly passed out of sight. Then my sister, in meek silence, led my horse, briddled and saddled, to the door and assisted me to mount, my crutches on one arm my wounded foot hanging straight down. Turning my horse towards the gate he leaped the fence; I felt that I was again for a time at least a free man. Going in the direction of a friend's house for whom they had inquired and knowing that, to get there first, I must go through the woods and ride rapidly, I pushed on and succeeded in warning the people to put their stock and themselves out of the way. This accomplished, I started in the direction of home and on going by to warn another Southern family of the raid that was upon them, I rode into this same crowd plundering the house of a Southern man; their horses tied along the yard fence; coming on to them in the manner in which I did it was almost impossible to go back. So I rode along by the fence, the men in the house looking at me but for some cause they hesitated and did not fire upon me. Trusting to my good horse, Texas, dangerous as it was I passed them; my beautiful gray horse whose action was good and of whose speed I had no doubt, I gave the word to go and he went by in such speed that in a moment of time I had passed and turned down the hill out of their sight and out of range of their shots. I continued my ride deep into the bottom. The wound in my foot by this time bled quite freely and it was considerably swollen by swinging down so long. When I was fully safe, I dismounted and remained two days before I was again able to move.

CHAPTER VIII.

A Reign of Terror.

Emerging from my seclusion I went back into the country where I could at least feel safe from the enemies of our country and get much needed rest. About this time came the fall of Richmond and the surrender of Lee's army which sounded the death knell of the Southern Cause. The Unionists became very much emboldened by this and became more and more aggressive towards their Southern neighbors and especially towards those who had been in the Southern army. Many of those who had been enlisted in the federal army from our part of the country began to return to their homes. Flushed with victory by the accomplishment of that towards which they had contributed very little, they banded together with a lot of scoundrels who had not been in the federal army, save for a spell, but who wore the blue for the purpose of murder, arson and theft. I remember well one calm summer day in 1865 when they went to the home of Dr. J. J. McBride, robbed the house of what they wanted and burned the premises and buildings with contents. Moving on from this they came to the house of Mr. Briggance, an old and respected citizen, whose only offense was that he had a son who had been in the Confederate army and who was then at home and at work on the farm. They marched this son to the house, tied him to a tree in the yard and in the presence of his aged father and mother shot him to death and burned the house and contents. Moving on in this work they nest came across Mr. George Swift. Him they murdered and left dead on the roadside for a pious father and mother to take home and bury. Proceeding on, the next victim was an old and inoffensive man, he, as the

others, had been a Confederate soldier; he too was shot down in his own doorway. These are only a few of the many occurrences of this kind that happened during that reign of terror. Looking back over these times my blood recoils at the recital. Some of this same crew of outlaws came to Mr. J. H. Galbraith's; his son, J. N. Galbraith, was at home on parole; his aged mother, young wife and little sister were present. They began to shoot at him; the pleadings of a mother, wife and sisters for the life of a dear one, pleading only as they could plead, had no effect on them. He fled; they pursued and shot at him. Being weak they soon overtook him. Being well acquainted with him, they said, "Newt, c---- you, we have a mind to kill you but will let you pass this time, you look so d---- bad. " This set of men had been, by him many times, accommodated, as a merchant and in many ways. This reign of terror continued on and on; about this time, the last of May and first of June, the paroled soldiers of the Confederate armies, that were left, began to arrive home. That remnant of the proudest army that ever faced a foe, many of whom had not seen home nor friends since 1861, without money, without clothes save a much worn and faded Confederate suit. They went to work with the same determination to make a crop as they had to win the fight. But even at this peaceful occupation with a parole ill their pockets, many of them were shot at their plows. Looking back over this reign of terror one can but exclaim, "Great God! dost Thou control and direct the destinies of men upon the earth?" On many occasions the ex-Confederates, at work; their old gray jackets would be taken off, and being on the fence or other convenient place while at work, if there chanced to pass a squad of these federals, they would frequently stop and draw their pistols and proceed to put the old jackets full of bullet holes. The ex- Confederates, unarmed and not allowed to carry arms, they would curse and abuse the ex-Confederates to their heart's content. This thing becoming so unbearable that there arose what was known as the Ku-Klux-Klan, a secret oath-bound organization among the Southern people. They wore masks and traveled in the night-time. The insignia was a skull and cross-bones. Of this order I was a loyal member and woe unto the insolent negro or turbulent white man who incurred its displeasure! This was made necessary in self defense and had the effect of putting a quietus on the insolence of that crew of thieves. By fall of the year my wound had so much improved that I had began to wear a soft shoe. In company with another rebel I repaired to another part of the country and began to build and repair cotton gins. We found our work in demand and prices remunerative; so we continued while there was work of that kind to do. That winter I went home and father and all of us went to work repairing his premises and rebuilding his mill which had gone down during the war. By the spring of 1866, I was sufficiently recovered to wear a shoe and began to clean up a piece of land which had not been cultivated but once during the war and was overgrown with bushes; many trunks of fallen trees still lay where they had fallen. I began, I think the first of February to cut and burn logs, dig grubs and fix fence with no help but my own hands, hoping that I might be able to make an honest living by the sweat of my face and be unmolested by those unprincipled scoundrels; but not so, by this time the whole of the federal army, which had been enlisted in this country had returned to their homes; their pockets lined with greenback money, good horses and good clothes. Many, in fact most of the ex- Confederates, having been driven from their homes or killed, it was thought too much for an ex-Confederate captain to live in that country; much less to have the audacity to attempt to till the earth and cultivate a crop. So I was again spotted as one not worthy to cumber the earth. The plans were laid that, on a certain Tuesday, I should pay the penalty by giving up my life as many others had done not long before.

I was hard at work chopping on a big, hard, old log and on looking up towards the road, I saw an old man, whom I recognized, as, having been at the beginning of the war in 1861, a rabid secessionist, but who had after the battle of Shiloh become extremely loyal to the other side, riding carelessly along eyeing me all the while. This gave me an uneasiness. Getting my horse and watching, I soon saw twenty-seven men in blue rushing towards me from every direction, halting and shooting at me all the while. It seemed for a little while that they had me, but, being astride my splendid gray horse, Texas, I rode out through them and made my escape without hurt or loss, except my hat and a rather painful wound in one shoulder caused by the horse running against a tree. There was no legal process out for my arrest or anything of that kind. They had been entertained at a citizen's house for a day or two, dancing, drinking etc., and to close the entertainment in good style, go out and kill a rebel, which they failed to do this time at least. Returning in a couple of days, I determined to make a crop or die in the field so proceeded with my work, keeping my faithful horse tied near me, a double barreled shotgun conveniently near and a pistol always at hand. When it came time to commence plowing, I plowed a mule, kept my horse bridled and saddled near the center of the field. At night I slept in the woods where I might be safe; neighbor boys frequently staying with me. On one occasion a man whom I had known well before the war by the name of John Griswell, came walking slowly into the field where I was at work. Allowing him to come within about forty yards of where I was, I put my hand on the gun and asked him if he wanted anything. "No, nothing much." he said with a yawn. "You seem to be pretty well armed," said he. "Yes, fairly well," I answered. "I just thought I would come down and see how you were getting on." "Thank you," said I, "won't you come nearer?"

"Thank you," said he, "I'll be going. Good-bye." I watched the receding figure with considerable mirth, though it was all by myself, and thought of the wolf that went out to get wool and came back shorn. He doubtless thought that he would come down, find me unarmed and do and say just what he pleased. Proceeding with my work I made about fifty barrels of corn and nearly one bale of cotton. The reign of terror still continuing, things had come to the point where I could not longer remain in the country without either killing a lot of them or being killed. I had at intervals worked a little in a country store and boarded with the proprietor, whose eldest daughter, then at home, was to my mind as perfect a model of Southern womanhood as could possibly be found and to say that I admired and loved her was putting it mildly. But to mention such a thing to her, situated as I then was, I could not afford to do. Through the advice of friends and considering a treacherous and unrelenting foe which I had to deal with, it was thought best that I leave the country. I accordingly bid the home-folks adieu and with a heavy heart parted with them all, and especially when it came to bidding farewell to her whom I loved and had not dared to tell so.

CHAPTER IX.

My Trip to Kentucky and Teaching School in Tennessee.

I went on my way to Kentucky; arriving there, I found many good, warm-hearted Southern people who gave me employment and treated me kindly. I went immediately to cutting wood at one dollar per cord all that winter and spring, driving a team part of the time. During the summer I went to school, worked Saturdays and all vacations, finally selling my horse and going to school more, obtaining a very limited education - arithmetic, geography and English grammar. Returning during the winter of 1868 to Henderson, Tenn., where I engaged as a clerk at a very small salary, more to learn the business than for the money which I was getting for it. At the expiration of my term of service for the firm. I was asked to teach a school at Center Point, my old home and neighborhood, which I gladly accepted. Matters had undergone a great change during these years. The Republican party, that party of corruption and oppression, had passed an act in 1861, disfranchising all Southern sympathizers and ex-Confederates, that is, not allowing them to vote nor hold office in the state, but the leaders of this same party had fallen out among themselves; one of them being governor and another one wishing to be; the one who was already governor, fearing the other one would defeat him and having the power to issue certificates of enfranchisement to whom he pleased, had his agents appointed and issued them broadcast; the result being his election by a large majority and the election of a democratic legislature also the enfranchisement of all the people. Thus was brought about the saying. "When thieves fall out, honest men get their dues. "Seeing the Democrats again in power in the state and this rabble having spent most of their war money, a good many of them having been killed, first and last, they were very much calmed down. Seeing their political rule at an end, they were quite willing for peace and friendship to which we assented. So I went on with my school two years, having good success, about as many pupils as I could attend to, many of them being young men and young women whose opportunities had been poor as had been my own. At the end of two years I had advanced the classes as far as I had education to do; so I closed out the school-teaching business, sat by the door and bid my pupils each farewell as they filed out and away with a strange sadness in my heart, wondering what would be the life of this one and that one. Let me say, though, in closing this chapter, that all of the boys and girls who were of my pupil, all of them save one, have made men and women of honor and integrity. Among their number today are some of the most successful farmers, merchants, doctors, etc., and for each and all of them I entertain the highest admiration and respect. Looking over my accounts I found that I had made after paying my little expenses, one thousand dollars, so I put forth my energies and collected it up. Not much money, you will say and tight too, but then I had made it honestly and saved it and it was my own, hence my appreciation.

CHAPTER X.

My Marriage and Business Career.

Turning my attention now, for something more permanent and lasting in the way of a business pursuit, than school- teaching, still having in mind the features of a brown-eyed, dark-haired maiden, before referred to, in fact, the image of her rosy cheeks, gentle voice and manners, had not faded from my memory during all these years. Time had rather intensified than weakened my admiration for her. So from what I had seen and heard on the subject, I concluded that I was really in love with Miss Mary S. Galbraith. Being now in the thirty-first year of my age and she in her twenty-first, thought we ought to get married. I proposed and she accepted accordingly. On the fourteenth day of Dec. 1871 we were united in marriage by Rev. Mr. Swift, a

Methodist minister, and a true Southern man. On the third day after our marriage, we took a bridal tour, walked about four hundred yards to her brothers, Mr. J. N. Galbraith's, home, took dinner, had a good time and returned, being pleased with the partnership already formed; I concluded to try a further partnership with the family in a business way; I conferred with Mr. Jno. H. Galbraith and his son J. N. Galbraith upon the subject, and after some deliberating, they agreed to accept me as a business partner. So with my one thousand dollars, I entered the mercantile business. Our business did fairly well. At the end of three years we thought best to dissolve the firm which we did. I then went into business on my own account, at the same place; of course in a very small way. I entered my own establishment which was a very small concern, being a log house 18x24 feet.

I succeeded fairly well, built up a good trade, and for eleven years worked faithfully and hard; as I now remember, losing only three or four days by sickness during these years. My business prospered as well as it could in a country place with only a small capital to operate upon. I worked all the while; if I thought it necessary to ride at night to see after my affairs, I did so, rain or shine; I failed not; how foolish! as the sequel will show. All this time my faithful wife was ever at my side, to aid, to comfort and to encourage. Her health was not very good. She was not strong, but looked well to the ways of her household, ate not the bread of idleness, and took special care of everything I made, rejoicing with me at our moderate success. Not knowing how the wealthy fared nor how the very poor lived, we were free from both extremes and as happy as we could well be. I am reminded of the saving of the prophet: "take me neither rich nor poor, lest I be rich and forget Thee, or poor and despise Thee." Our oldest son now being about eleven years old and our only daughter about eight, we thought it necessary to see about their education and having no school at or near our home at Center Point, we decided best for the children that we go to Henderson, the county seat of our county, where we might educate our children. Our youngest child, a boy, having died in infancy left us only the two children, Thos. B. and Vorena H. Carroll. Accordingly we purchased a lot and built a house, wife and children moved to it, the children entering school. I continued my business at Center Point, but during the second year of this mode of living, my health began to give way. Suffering from the effects of wounds which brought on a disease known among the physicians as locomotor ataxia from which I will never recover; having been most of the time since I was attacked, a period of fourteen years, only able to do a very little work and now for the past six months have not been out of my door-yard but one time.

Our children did well in school. Thos. B. graduated in West Tennessee Christian College, married when about twenty- one years of age to Miss Suzelle Murchison, a beautiful and accomplished lady. They have two sons, Raymond Trice and John Murchison Carroll, of whom I am very proud.

CHAPTER XI.

The Only Daughter.

Our daughter, Vorena H., graduated at the West Tennessee Christian College. We then sent her to a female college at Holly Springs, Miss., for two years, where she added to her former acquirements. She was not a thorough scholar, but liberally educated in languages - English, French and German; a full course of mathematics, music and art; in all of which she did well; added to these were all the household acquirements necessary. And above all of a noble character, amiable disposition, a kind word for all, the humble as well as the favored. Our extreme love for her was fully reciprocated. During her absence at school, we built a new house on our lot and otherwise beautified our home. On her return from school she said, "Papa, this is the prettiest place on earth. I never want to leave here again." We were all so happy at being together once again. We thought she was with us to remain to cheer us along down the shady side of life. But alas! She was not to be. After only a few months she was stricken with that awful disease, peritonitis, from which she lingered eight and a half months in great pain. All that medical science could do was done. The best nursing in our power and that of a host of friends was rendered, but all to no avail. Death, the grim monster, that calls alike for the good and the bad, the innocent and the guilty, came and took her from us. At the awful stroke, the light seemed to have gone out of our home and happiness departed from the earth as far as we were concerned. A small marble enclosure, a plat of green grass, a few flowers and evergreens, planted there by loving hands, in the Henderson cemetery, mark the spot where we laid to rest our loving and beloved daughter, whose remains must await the call of the resurrection. Her photo on the mantel, her works of art on the walls, her little room, her everything left, only reminded us more forcibly of the departed one whom we shall never more see upon the earth. Anything and everything of hers we see are only silent reminders of her industrious hands and amiable disposition.

CHAPTER XII.

My Subsequent Business and Advice.

Let me now drop back a few years to the beginning of my ill health and bad luck. Being prostrated as I before referred to, I was taken to Henderson and in the spring following hauled back to Center Point, spending the summer there and selling half interest in my business to J. R. Washburn and later selling him the other half. Returning to Henderson I engaged in business with W. E. McCleod. Later we took in another partner, Mr. W. G. Massengill; later we dissolved this firm. Still later I engaged in business with Mr. W. C. McCollum. Our business did not prosper, losing heavily on cotton, in fact almost everything. At this time, the general government forcing a gold standard upon the country, ruined us financially. I went out of the business, but not out of debt. Shrinkage in values of everything at a ruinous rate; cotton going down from 11 cents per pound to 4 1/2 to 6; corn from 65 cents per bushel to 16 cents; real estate declining at least 300 percent; good lands in the vicinity of Henderson which brought from 25 to 40 dollars per acre, twelve years before, could not now be sold at all for more than six to ten dollars per acre. Business men, the oldest, best traders of all kinds, going into insolvency right along one after another; creditors becoming more and more exacting; syndicates and banking institutions becoming more and more cautious, exacting 12 per cent. and 15 per cent. for the use of money; a pound of money or a pound of flesh seemed to be the order of the day and holders of real estate who like myself thought it the safest and best collateral in the world, found themselves suddenly bankrupt. The products of the soil going at such low prices, the people actually became too poor to consume. In this condition I find not only myself but many others and when the end will come or what will be the final result, I cannot foretell. If it does not end in revolution I shall be agreeably surprised. Under this system of government, the money-lender is in position to demand of the producer, who has to have money, about as much of the products of the soil as he wants for a dollar. In many cases this is so. I claim that we are entitled to an equal chance in the race of life; no more, no less. That when the government steps in and says by law to the holder of real estate, "I will reduce the volume of currency so that money will become scarce and high and everything else;" or in other words it shall take 2 1/2 pounds of cotton to bring as much money as 1 pound did three years ago, or four acres of land, or three horses;

this is simply highway robbery, no less so because done under the forms of law. Government has put forth its hands and taken from one of its citizens and given to another, because that other had invested in bonds and gold while the one had put his money into real estate, thereby reducing the wealth of two-thirds to three-fourths and enhancing the wealth of the other in like proportion. Such is the case in this country today and the government which did it ought to be reformed or abolished, laying its foundation on better principles. Thomas Jefferson said, "Equal and exact justice to all, special privileges to none," which is the only true policy of government.

Now in this year of grace, by observation and experience I am prepared to offer the following suggestions. I am persuaded that I am correct when I say, look well to your health, guard it with a zealous care. That is your only capital. Fortunately for you, maybe, you were not born rich, but what is better, you were born of healthful parents, having sound bodies and strong minds. Of which we hope you have inherited much. Having that grand prerequisite to begin with, you have it within your power to rise to positions of trust and eminence.

Merit being the card that always wins in the end, therefore prepare yourselves to fill any position to which you may be called and, when called, discharge it faithfully and fully to the very utmost detail, be that position high or low. Should you become farmers, lawyers, or teachers, it matters not what your calling may be, stand at the head of the list; try to be the very best. Remember that success is obtained only by a thorough knowledge of, and close application to, every detail of a business. Be sure to ask of those who are proficient in any business or study that you would like to learn. They could perhaps give you in a few words what it would perhaps take you weeks, unaided, to learn.

"Seize upon truth wherever found;
Be it upon Christian or heathen ground."

In you intercourse with the world be ever so courteous to all, especially to the aged. It is worth all it costs and more too. "Bow thyself to the hoary head and honor the face of the old man," saith the scriptures.

Don't ever think that the eyes of older persons are not looking upon you and taking cognizance of your conduct. For there certainly will be others besides father and mother who will do this, and the estimate placed upon you by these outside persons will determine largely your standing in the community. Much depends upon this.

Be sure never to deceive any one. Speak the truth though the heavens' fall. Be ever careful to do only such acts as you would be neither ashamed nor afraid for the world to know. Then you will be all right. A conscience void of offense is the great bulwark to manhood. In fact you can never be manly men if your lives are flecked with deeds of evil.

Should you with friends at any time' enter into any kind of contest in school work' or anything else, do your best in an honorable way and, if successful, never arrogate to yourself all the praise for the success, but concede to those who worked with you full honor for their part. Modesty, that crowning gem of the virtues, demands this of you. It will make personal friends of the one you' thus act toward. Some civilities of this sort, especially towards the poor or those whose station in life might be below yours, will be appreciated and make them your friends. Whereas an abrupt speech or haughty manner will make them enemies. You want the friendship of all, where it is not necessary to sacrifice principle to obtain it. This never do under any circumstances.

Have few confidants outside of father and mother, but should you have, which most persons do, be a confidant indeed; keep locked within your own bosom anything thus communicated to you if you thus agree. It is in many cases better, though, to say, to one who seems to have a great secret he wishes to communicate, that you prefer that he does not tell you. It is such an easy matter to become a tattler if one is not particular.

You are certain to have troubles that you want sympathy and help to solve. In such time go to father and mother who are your best friends and into whose ears you can confidently pour all your hopes and fears and whose experience in life and observation of men and things, will enable them to point you in an honorable way out of your troubles. Depend upon them and take their advice. In them you have friends without dissimulation, variableness, or shadow of turning. The world may buffet you, pass by, and scoff at your misfortunes. Men, who in your days of prosperity were ever ready to smile upon you, many times in your hours of distress will not know you. All men will not do this but some men will. Father and mother never will, consequently go to them. Tell them the trouble, take their advice, their experience in life will enable them to point out to you the dangers in this or that course; also to direct you what to run after and what to refrain from; that which is dangerous to your life and character, also that which will be ennobling to both.

To mother be very kind, respectful and obedient. She will never forsake you. Prison bars might enclose you, which God forbid, but even then mother will be there to own, to comfort, and to plead for her sons. If necessary to go to the very death, she will go for you. Having such how kind, obedient and careful you should ever be toward her. If mother is sick, wait upon her; nurse her; care for her. On rising in the morning never fail to seek mother and say: "Mother, are you well today?" Never leave home even for one day without telling father and mother good-bye; and on returning never fail to greet them kindly. They will appreciate this in you more than you suspect. They entertain for your welfare a deep solicitude; the depth and intensity of which you have but little idea. Be ever kind to all people, especially those in distress; despise no one's condition in life, for think to-day how sad or poor may be yours tomorrow.

CHAPTER XIII.

"Be Ye Temperate in All Things." - Bible.

This as well as all the teachings of Scripture, when properly considered and correctly understood, leads its followers in paths of peace and beside still waters and maketh them to lie down in green pastures.

Be Temperate In Eating.

He that gormandizes makes himself sick, enlarges his stomach, taxes his digestive organs above their capacity; a sluggish feeling follows. Dyspepsia and other kindred diseases follow and last but not least a slow, dull, incomprehensive intellect. Avoid this.

Be Temperate In Work.

Never undertake to do in one hour that which would require two hours; for if you do you will not do the work as it should be done. You will exhaust your strength in a flurry and perhaps require a whole day to recuperate. Don't do this. Remember that to complete a certain amount of work ordinary mortals require time and pains, and that the same time is required for you. Make it a rule of your life to do well that which you undertake. It always pays in the end. Besides if you establish a reputation of doing well that which you undertake, you will seldom, if ever, be out of something to do. Whereas on the other hand, if you turn off shoddy work, it matters not what line, your services will not be wanted.

Be Temperate In Expression.

I have so often heard extravagant expressions that I wondered that someone didn't take them to task about it. I have heard such expression from right sensible persons too: "As high as a tree," "as black as a negro," etc., when the objects spoken of did not resemble trees nor negroes; neither did the persons speaking intend to be so understood. How much better to express ourselves in moderation! Be exact as possible; never exaggerate in your description. Then explanations are unnecessary.

Be sure to govern your passions in a proper manner. Why, I have heard persons say, "I got so mad at so-and-so, or such- and-such persons" - as if to fly into a passion was a virtue that all might be proud of. Such a one has my sympathy; a terrible malady has possessed him instead of a virtue. Why, a man in extreme anger, a drunk man and a crazy man are for the time being much alike. They are unfitted for business, unfitted for social circles, a torture to themselves, unpleasant to their friends, in fact repulsive to all. Therefore how important it is maintain an equal frame of mind, thereby being at all times ready for the transaction of business, the reception of friends and for the practice of morality and virtue.

Above all avoid the intemperate use of ardent spirits. In fact use it not at all. Intoxicating drinks are harmful to all, and, when once a person has become habituated to the use of this stimulant, it is frequently impossible for him to resist the temptation. Many a good boy and bright young fellow can note the beginning of his downward career to his first drink. Never take the first one and you will never need the second. Never begin drinking the vile stuff and you will never have to quit. Let it severely alone. If you drink it to excess, which you may do, if you drink at all, it will corrupt your morals however good, cause you to waste your time and money; it will cause you to be shunned by the good and virtuous; it will make your wife a slave and your children beggars; it will ruin the happiness of your home, dethrone your reason and make you hate yourself; it will leave your boys and girls uneducated and paupers; it causes suicides, beggars, murderers, and, if there is anything else imaginable more horrible, it is that also. Never go near such damnable places as where whiskey is sold. How easy it is for persons in both youth and age to become entangled in the meshes of intemperance! Go not near it. Go nowhere or into no place where you would be ashamed for your mother or sister to go, or where you would be ashamed to be found dead. Never play cards nor gamble in any way. It leads to ruin; and remember, when you have staked your first money on any game or taken the first drink, you have taken the first step in a downward course-boys, never take it.

In your business relations with men be careful that you fully understand the propositions and that the person with whom you are trading understands every detail as well as yourself. This will prevent misunderstandings and lawsuits, make lasting friends, and keep you out of much trouble. Make promises slowly and after much deliberation and then not without you see some reasonable chance of fulfillment. But when you have promised, bend all your energies to make your word good. Never go to law about trifles; it is better to sustain a small loss than to enter into lawsuits. The winner in such cases is loser in the end. Avoid every appearance of wrong-doing and all appearance of evil or that which might lead to misunderstandings.

Should you enter into mercantile pursuits, be careful to take care of yourself. Go not in debt. Buy only what you can pay for at the time or on very short notice. Sell' for the money and, should you owe anything, pay it out of the first money. Remember that should you get behind - owe matured bills that you cannot meet, no one will come to your relief, except that he is to get more from you that he gives. You will have in this, as in all other things in life, to stand alone, unaided, and the sooner you realize this fact the better for you. Therefore begin in that way.

Beware of debt; shun it as you would the deadly upas-tree. Anyone out of debt is in pretty fair condition. Earn your money with your hands. When you have done this, you will the more appreciate it and be the better prepared to make paying investments. Knowing the amount of labor that is necessary to earn a dollar, you will know exactly what a dollar is worth and, therefore, look the closer to your interests and let matters which do not concern you, especially, pass by; for should you espouse the cause of everyone who has a grievance, your time will be so closely occupied with other people's business that your own affairs will suffer thereby.

Always have as soon as it is possible for you to earn it, a small amount of cash on hand, that you may be able to take advantage of any good trade that is offered. Such trades come to those who have ready money. Any person man or boy, with one dollar in his pocket, though his clothes be patched and his hat seedy, is in better conditon and much to be preferred to the conditon of the one who has no money and who is "diked" up in good clothes and owes for them. The first one is a free man; the second, a slave.

In selecting your associates prefer those whose moral and intellectual acquirements are high; and to be congenial and companionable to such associates, it will be incumbent upon you to prepare yourself to entertain them in conversation upon such topics as are interesting to them. This will require at your hands attention to your reading, study of history, biography, travels, etc., not neglecting the current literature of the day. No one enjoys the society of another whom they know to be their inferior in point of culture. Therefore, should you aspire to associate with well-informed persons, you must also be informed, and then cultivate the art of being a good listener as well as a good conversationalist. Should there be one in your midst who is backward or timid, manage by gentle means to draw him into the conversation; he will perhaps give you a lot of information. Modesty, being one of the cardinal virtues, should be respected. Should one of your company be speaking, listen attentively until he has finished; then give your views, if at all, in a plain, simply unostentatious manner. Let the company see that you are not vain nor puffed up. Should you enter into discussion with anyone upon any question either for information or because you consider his position an erroneous one, do so in a calm and dignified manner. And in stating the position of an opponent, state it correctly and fairly, but discuss its features with all you ability and with all the proof of history, or testimony that you can command and expect the same of him. In your debating societies it is better to trust your memory as to statements of an opponent than to write notes. The former will so much improve your memory as to enable you after a time to repeat almost a whole speech, whereas, writing tends to weaken the memory. Therefore, cultivate your memory in every way possible. Commit to memory songs, poetry, speeches of able men, whole chapters of Scripture for you will find it will pay you. With this fund of information on hand, you can call it to your aid at will; you will surely need it. The historian, Gibbon, it is said, could commit to memory a whole page of the London Times by breakfast. This came largely by cultivation. Do likewise. In your selection of books read none but those of standard authors. Dime novels and other trashy reading tend to weaken the understanding. Have nothing to with them. If your associates are those who have nothing to talk about higher than neighborhood gossip or scandal, if we hear that alone, we will soon be of the same mental calibre and look, listen, and enquire for more of the same abominable stuff.

Just so with or reading; we must cultivate a desire for the best, right at the start before our minds become vitiated by the absorption of evil. Always, in conversation, speak of things more than of persons. If you can speak well of anyone, do so in moderation; if you cannot thus speak, it is best to remain silent. If it should be necessary for you to speak in condemnation of the acts of any one, be kind enough to say perhaps the man may be pretty fair but his act was bad. Judge not harshly of anyone for you perhaps are not fully aware of all his surroundings. Environments have much to do with the deeds of all of us; therefore let us be mild in our condemnation until we know all the facts.

CHAPTER XIV.

Incidents in the Life of Jack Briggance.

Mr. Briggance was a true Southern man and, when after the battle of Shiloh the whole of West Tennessee was overrun by the federals and when the loyal unionists of our own country were extremely troublesome, it became unsafe for Jack to remain at home. So resorting to cover of the woods and night to save his life, he became somewhat noted as a guerrilla. Many were the federals that he captured, unaided and alone, and carried across to Middle Tennessee or other places where he could deliver them to the Confederate authorities. When he had delivered one, he lost no time but would immediately return under cover of darkness and bring forth another lot. On one such tour, traveling until late in the night before he came to the federal camp, the weather being very warm and raining all night, Jack was very tired and sleepy; so much so that on his return with his prisoner he became so fatigued that he called at the house of a friend for a short rest. Telling the Yankee to lie down and rest, which the fellow seemed very anxious to do; after a few minutes Jack dropped asleep. The Yankee immediately took the gun, tapped Jack on the shoulder and told him, "We will now return to camp." Jack dreaded this very much, but there was no chance but to accept. After marching back a couple of hours, the Yankee became very tired and proposed to stop in out of the rain and wait until daylight. Briggance of course assented. This time Jack went to sleep and the Yank was guard. Pretty soon, the Yank went to sleep and Briggance took the gun, woke him and told him they would now return towards the land of Dixie. This time he landed him on the east side of the Tennessee river where the Confederate forces took charge of him.

The Writer's Experience.

Away back in 1866 when it was decided unsafe for me to remain longer in my native country, I decided to go to Kentucky. On my way, passing through Dyersburg, Tenn., I concluded to exchange my cavalry saddle with a saddler for one of a more peaceful and citizen-like look. While at this, a lot of ex-federal soldiers surrounded my horse and began to say, "I know that horse," which I knew was not so. But, as their custom was, I thought they intended to take him from me by force if necessary. I went on putting on my new saddle, adjusting the length of the stirrup, etc., until I was ready to mount; pulling a navy six which I had attached to a belt and hid under all overcoat well to the front, I announced boldly that,

"This is my horse, gentlemen," mounted and rode away, but not without many misgivings as to what might befall me before night. Occasionally looking back to see if I was being pursued, I pushed on finally coming to the Obion river and near Hale's Point on the Mississippi river. Dark came on me. Finding the Obion river three miles wide from the backwater and no means of crossing that night, I sought a place to remain over night. I wanted a private place too, so, if pursued, I might not be found. Turning my horse into a bridle path leading along near the water's edge, I soon came to what had once been a substantial residence; darkness now had fully closed upon everything. Calling at the fence, a man answered and upon inquiring if I could pass the night with him, said I could but would have to occupy the same bed with him, to which I assented. Alighting, he ordered a darkey to take my horse and put him away. There was quite a number of negroes about there and when my horse was being led away, I never expected to see him again, but of that I spoke not to my host. We entered the cabin. Pretty soon a negro woman brought in a supper of bacon and cornbread. Soon the table was put back. The room being only about sixteen feet square, containing one bed, a table, one large box, was quite full. Soon the negroes whom I soon found occupied all the other buildings on the place, began to file into the cabin. Mr. Selph (for such was his name) reached for an old fiddle and began playing a kind of mixture between "Mollie Put the Kettle On" and "Run, Negroes, Run." These negroes dancing with all their might and eyeing the stranger with peculiar inquisitveness. Jim would jump as high as the table while Bill and Joe cut the pigeon wing. Sal was good on the back-step; other ladies of the crew did equally well. All of which I feigned to admire and especially the music. Thus, the party went on, enjoyed as they supposed very much by me in whose honor I suppose it was given. I swayed with the music and heaped encouragement on Jim, my object being to keep it going all night if possible. I thought by doing so they probably would not steal my horse. About ten o'clock at night a couple of men came to the fence and calling Mr. Selph to them held a hurried conversation. Returning he invited me and insisted that I should accompany them about a mile where they said a very entertaining time might be had. To this I demurred and insisted that our own party proceed. The men disappearing the dance proceeded. While Selph was out, I took a survey of things and saw a carbine and brace of pistols hanging on the wall beside a federal uniform, which was anything but reassuring to me. I soon saw he was tired of his fiddling and without assistance in music the pleasure would cease. So I seized the instrument, gave it a few jerks and proceeded to accommodate the crowd with "Big Nigger Rare Around," which must be heard to be appreciated. This enlivened Jim and the other dancers to such a pitch, that I really thought the entertainment would last all night, Mr. Selph himself finally taking a hand in the dance. However about two o'clock a.m., Sunday, as it now was, we decided, not on account of it being Sunday but on account of being worn out, to quit for the night. The negroes repaired to their cabins and mine host and I began to discuss matters a little. Observing my coat was of Confederate gray, I told him frankly I had been a Confederate soldier. He told me he had once been also, but had gone to the federals and had deserted them also. So we retired, he going to bed first and behind and I, on the front side. He put his pistol under his head; I drew mine and laid it on a box at my head. He went to sleep but I did not. I imagined a great many things; many of which might have been true if I had just but known. Of one thing I was certain, I was in the presence of and in the house of one of the worst wrecks of humanity I had ever met. There among those negroes he lived an outcast I felt certain. No other white person on the premises and a lot of ferocious looking negro bucks to do his bidding. I felt I would be in luck to get away, but felt somewhat reassured from my performance on the violin. Daylight soon came, though, and to my delight and surprise I found my horse all right; I had a meat-and-bread breakfast; I was a splendid fellow with mine host as well as with the negroes. I engaged the negroes to ferry me across the backwater three miles, which they did; paid my bills; bid Mr. Selph a goodbye, promising to return and spend another night with him on first passing, which I have never done yet and guess never will.

War Incidents of Mr. (afterwards Lieutenant) M. L. of My Company.

About the winter of 1862 after the battle of Shiloh, the federals having taken possession of West Tennessee and especially the river counties and many of those who had been rabid secessionists only a short time before; and many others who thought more of greenback money, a suit of blue clothes and a horse, which they never paid for, than they did of their country, entered the Federal army, not for the good of the service; not that they ever expected to fight the Confederate forces; but for the sole purpose of terrorizing their

Southern neighbors. Such a one was Jack Jones, who upon seeing Mr. Cherry go into the house of a miller to whose mill he had gone to get meal for his family, rode up to the dooryard fence and thus accosted Mr. Cherry: "Come out here, Mr. Cherry. By God I am northern cavalry. I have come to take you off, you G--- d--- rebel." Cherry said, "Jack, I don't see how I can go today; my wife and children need some meal." "Get over the fence, I tell you," said Jones as he reared up in his stirrups. "All right," said Cherry, "if I must, I will." So proceeding to the fence, and stepping over he seized a hoe and dealt Jones such a blow across the side of the head as brought him to the ground and then proceeded to give him such a beating as only a large stout man thoroughly aroused, could do. The old miller all the while begging for Jones' life, and knowing full well that, if Jones was killed there at his door, perhaps his own life would be the forfeit. He finally persuaded Cherry to leave Jones alive, when the following dialogue ensued:

Cherry - "Jack Jones, if I spare your life this time, will you ever insult me again?"

Jones - "No, I will not, Mr. Cherry."

Cherry - "Jack, if you ever meet another man that looks like I do, will you meddle with him?"

Jones - "I will not, Mr. Cherry."

Cherry - "If I conclude not to cut your head off with this hoe and throw it away, will you ever be seen in this country again, Jack."

Jones - "No sir, Mr. Cherry, I will not."

Cherry then permitted the miller to assist Jones on his horse and he moved off, his new federal uniform stained in his own blood, and his head and face much battered and so far as I know he kept his word and was never seen in that part of the country again.

How a Bride of Twenty-four Hours Out-talked a Rebel Colonel and Liberated Her Husband.

During the winter of 1862-3 there was a great effort made on the part of the Confederates to gather in absentees and, to further this end, recruiting stations were established at every place where we could hold a position bordering on territory held by the enemy. Accordingly a station of this sort was established at Linden, Tenn. A Mr. Appleby, who was a member of the 27th Tenn. Reg., had left the command without permission and gone out on the west side of the Tennessee river. Hearing of his whereabouts and that he was to be married on the east side of the river on a certain night, the commandant of the post, Col. Frierson, sent a squad of soldiers to the place to arrest Mr. Appleby. Arriving on the premises about 9 p.m., we found the marriage ceremony had been performed. The entertainment - music and dancing - was going on in high glee. Arresting the newly-married gentleman, we started immediately to Linden with him; arriving there we delivered him to the Colonel who of course ordered him to the guard-house for safe keeping. On the following evening the bride appeared before the Colonel commanding the post; looking quite bright and pretty she said, "Colonel, you have my husband under guard. I am here to ask his release. I suppose you have a wife at home." "Yes, madam," replied the Colonel.

"Well, would you not consider it all act of cruelty to your wife to say nothing of yourself, were someone to lock you up in prison in sight of your home and in sight of her whom you loved, and deny you the pleasure of each other's company?" The Colonel hesitated, stammered, and coughed a little; his military dignity subsiding much and replied, "My dear madam, it would seem a little bad, but then military law - " "Hold on, colonel," replied the lady, "you have the law ill your hands in this case. I ask as a matter of justice that you release to me my husband." "Well, madam," replied he, "If your husband will agree to report every morning at nine o'clock while we are here. I will give an order for his release." "All right," responded the lady, "have him brought in." This was done, the husband, happy; the lady, in smiles; the military dignity at this time all gone out of the colonel. Upon leaving them the

Colonel said to the lady, "Now, if your husband should not report promptly, I shall have to take you in his place." "All right, Colonel, if my husband is not here at the proper time, I will be here in his place." So saying the couple departed. On the morrow at 9 a.m. the lady entered the office of the Colonel, looking her prettiest and said: "Well, Colonel, I told you if my husband did not report at the office this morning that I would; so here I am. Husband and I decided that he could do better over in West Tennessee or Kentucky than he could in the Confederate army. Colonel, what will you have me do?" The Colonel who, at this recital, had assumed all his military dignity appeared as though he wanted to fight something or somebody, but seeing how completely he had been out-generaled, said with a smile, "Madam, you will have to go." "Thank you, Colonel," replied the lady. As she passed out the door saying to the colonel, "Should you ever pass our way, come and see us. I am sure Mr. Appleby would appreciate entertaining you." And with a triumphant wave of her hand, she departed.

END.